Smarty Pig

By Molly Nero

Illustrator: Monique Turchan

Halo ●●●●
Publishing International

Paperback ISBN 13: 978-1-61244-048-4
Library of Congress Control Number: 2011919388

Printed in the United States of America

Halo ●●●●
Publishing International

Published by Halo Publishing International
AP·726
P.O. Box 60326
Houston, Texas 77205
Toll Free 1-877-705-9647
www.halopublishing.com
www.holapublishing.com
e-mail: contact@halopublishing.com

I want to thank my husband, Bernie who never stopped believing in me and my amazing kids, Claire and Nicolas. Without them and all the nights of reading together, I would never have started on this journey.

-Molly

It's well into the school year and as usual at night,
the piggies' house is hopping, no studying in sight.

There are piggies watching TV, and piggies playing cards.
Others have grabbed flashlights to play tag out in the yard.

Their backpacks are all heaped in a pile by the door
with homework papers crumpled up and folders on the floor.

But looking close, one tiny light is on up in the attic.
A little red-haired piggy is beginning to get frantic.

A project's due tomorrow. She had to get things going:
a colored map of Europe with all the countries showing.

Colored pencils scattered 'round with paper ready too,
she'd finished all her sketches and knew just what to do.

To her side, a notebook held a list of words to spell.
Next to it, lay a math test marked: "A+ You're doing well!"

The novel *Harry Piggy* sat with her book report begun.
The page to read held open with a bookmark: *READ FOR FUN!*

At nine fifteen in pink PJs, she snuggled into bed.
With noises all around, she put a pillow on her head.

The other piggies giggled as she studied while she ate.
Flicking corn pops in her book and tossing napkins on her plate.

They teased calling her, "Smarty Pig!" and "You're a Teacher's Pet!"
She ignored them all and focused on the good grades she would get.

Several weeks later, their report cards finally came.
All the other piggies hung their heads down in shame.

On each of their report cards, a red F filled each space.
They had flunked every subject. They were a disgrace.

"I just don't understand Math, and I really, really tried!
When I subtract, it doesn't work," one teary piggy cried.

"It's just not fair! My spelling words are hard," another whined.
"My Science projects never work. I'm just not the smart kind."

"What does it matter anyway? We'll never use this stuff.
They make us learn it just for tests." His voice was rather gruff.

Just then, that red-haired piggy walked with pride into the room.
Her report card had all A's and her smile brightened the gloom.

"To say that you don't need these skills, well that just isn't right.
You have to read and know Math facts for many things in life."

"How come you always get good grades?" they all began to ask.
"What do you do?"
"Can you show us?"
"Please help me with my Math!"

"It's really not that hard and I'll help you all I can.
But first, you must agree to try your best to understand.

I'll need markers and those cards, some beads, and a ball,
that play money from Pigopoly. The game is in the hall.
Up in the attic find the globe, the ruler, and my doll.
Grab the scale from the bathroom. Run quick and get them all.
We'll get started right away. Come on! It can be fun.
You'll learn it. I promise. We'll get the job done."

So the smart red-haired piggy who thought school was the best
was now appointed tutor to help teach all the rest.

In the kitchen, she took charge. "First open all the drawers.
Get food out of the pantry. We'll make it like a store."

On cards, she marked prices like groceries in town:
5 cents for each egg, apples 10 cents a pound.

She gave each pig play money with a small paper bag.
"Now count up the amount, so you know how much you have.
Pick out things to buy and go pay the amount.
Our cashier will give change. Just subtract and then count."

Off to the dining room that piggy she did dash.
Clearing off the table, she said, "Here is Science class."

She grabbed cooking oil, lotion and water from the kitchen,
measuring cups, spoons and bowls to put with them.

"I want you to think of which ones will mix best.
A hypothesis is just what you guess.
Now measure each one. Be exact. Take it slow.
It's like working with a recipe when making cookie dough.
Mix them together. See whose guess was right.
Some will mix; others won't. Try to find out why.

When you're finished cleaning up, the next thing we will do
is guess and weigh all these items I put out for you.
The chocolate cookies we all love, each weigh one gram.
Try to even out the scale as closely as you can."

From the kitchen came a squeal, "I get it now! I do!
Subtraction isn't very hard. Come watch. I'll help you too!"

Peering 'round the corner, she smiled ear to ear
watching the excited pigs take turns to be cashier.

She grabbed a bag of Piggy-O's as she walked through the door
and dumped out a small pile on the living room floor.

The youngest piggy worked as they sat with plastic string,
each one making pattern necklaces of pink, red and green.

This little one's next task: have 10 pieces on a mat.
She put 2 in his mouth and said, "Now that's how you subtract."

The little pig laughed and he smiled big with glee.
He finally understood that Math could really be easy.

The piggies loved each station and the games that she made.
They forgot about the skills that were practiced as they played.

Our little red-haired piggy was thrilled to help each day.
The pigs worked really hard and started getting better grades.

Instead of bad report cards and sullen, grumpy faces,
they loved to learn with A's and B's filling all those spaces.

Now that their "Smarty Pig" makes studying skills a game, the TV at night is silent but there's laughing just the same.

Experiments in the kitchen and Math games down the hall, they know now it's important. In life, you use it all.

CPSIA information can be obtained
at www.ICGtesting.com
Printed in the USA
258676LV00002B